Lesbian Erotic Short Story

A Gentle BDSM Adventure

Amber Carden

Chapter 1 - The Encounter 3
Chapter 2 BDSM Exploration 18
Chapter 3 The Pleasure 55

Chapter 1 - The Encounter

Elena has always been fascinated by BDSM, even as a little girl. Despite the fact that she has always been captivated by the complicated dance of power dynamics and control, she has never been able to find the ideal person with whom she can go into these dreams. Even though her past relationships were good in many ways, they were missing the passion and depth she wanted. Elena wants a partner who can help her understand her wants and limits more deeply and help her get through the complicated parts of BDSM.

Elena ends up at a secret LGBTQ+ club one night. The club is known for its lively vibe and diverse group of customers. People who want to be themselves can go to the club, which is a safe space where limits are pushed and new experiences are welcomed.

Elena looks around the room while sipping her drink at the bar. The pounding music and low lights create an electrifying environment, and she can feel the energy of the room being absorbed into her. She becomes aware of a group of ladies who are dancing in the vicinity of the center of the room. Their motions and laughs are carefree and uncontrolled. Even though she is in a very busy place, Elena can't help but feel that something big is going to happen.

While turning to drink more of her beverage, Elena fixes her gaze on a lady standing across the room. Sophia. Sophia is a charming and skilled dominatrix who is in her fifties. People are quickly drawn to her powerful personality and keen eyes. She has been a part of the BDSM community for years, which has helped her improve her skills and knowledge of power and control. Sophia's calm mood and deep look are the perfect mix of sexuality and power.

Sophia loves being in charge and the complicated dance of being in charge and being ruled over. Her skill as a dominatrix is clear from the way she carefully and carefully runs her lessons. She makes sure that her partners feel safe and understood because she believes in the power of trust and openness. She is very good at reading her partners and changing based on what they need, which makes each session unique and very fulfilling.

Sophia is a dominatrix, but she is also a complex person with a full and interesting life. She reads a lot, likes fine arts, and is very interested in psychology. All of these things help her understand people's wants and actions very well. Her close companions respect her intelligence and charm, and they often come to her for help with different issues.

Sophia's time in the BDSM world has given her strength and helped her understand herself better. She is known for being honest and loving the lifestyle, which has made her a trusted and loved person. Sophia sees BDSM as more than just power. It's also about relationship and respecting each other. She wants to be with people who are open to exploring their inner needs and who understand the careful balance between trust and power that is BDSM. Sophia's powerful energy can be felt even from far away. Her confident and authoritative demeanor and sharp eyes give her the impression that she can see Elena's spirit. From the moment Sophia locks eyes with Elena, a bond is forged, and the duration of their look seems endless.

Sophia starts to move through the crowd. She does this slowly and gracefully. Elena's heart is racing with a mix of joy and fear as she gets closer. She can feel how intense the moment is and how amazing something is about to happen.

Sophia says, "Hello," with a smooth, pure voice. "My name is Sophia."

She responds, "Hello, my name is Elena," but her voice is hardly discernible above the continuous music that is playing.

Sophia smiles, which is both friendly and powerful. "Elena, it's nice to meet you. What brings you here tonight?"

Elena tries to calm down by taking a deep breath. "I guess I'm just looking around. This place has gotten a lot of attention.

Sophia gives Elena a nod and keeps her eyes on her. "Yes, it is a unique place. With lots of options."

Sophia's confidence and charm make the talk run easily, and Elena is drawn to her. There is a lot of talk about their hobbies, adventures, and things that interest them. Sophia's stories keep Elena interested, and her vast knowledge and experience in the BDSM world both scare and attract her.

As the evening wears on, Sophia draws nearer to her, her voice a low whisper that is alluring. "Would you prefer to continue this discussion in another place private?"

Her heart beats faster. There is no doubt that she has been invited, and the thought of what lies ahead makes her feel both excited and scared. "Yes, I would," she says, her voice calm even though her chest is beating fast.

Sophia smiles, and her eyes show that she is happy. "Then follow me."

As they leave the club, the cool night air is very different from how hot and lively it was inside. Sophia leads Elena to a sleek black car that is waiting at the curb. Though the drive is short, it is very quiet, and the expectation grows with each second that goes by.

Sophia took her car to the building's parking lot and walked to her apartment when Elena and Sophia got there. Elena had caught up with her. They got into the main lift of the building. Elena is getting more and more excited as the lift makes its way to the top floor of the building. The apartment, which is high above the busy city streets, offers a private and stylish space. A stylishly appointed lobby with smooth marble flooring and gentle, ambient lighting that creates a lovely glow over the room is revealed when the doors are opened by the entrance.

Sophia shows Elena how to get into the loft and into the main living area. With windows that go from floor to ceiling, the room is very large and has a great view of the city below. The style is modern and simple, and the rich, dark wood paneling looks great against the lighter colors of the furniture. A few carefully chosen works of art and soft, low-slung chairs create a sophisticated and calm atmosphere.

With her smooth steps, Sophia leads them to a door that is set off to the side of the living room. When she opens it, she sees a room that is both warm and intense—it's meant for exploring the secrets of BDSM.

Sophia looks at Elena with a cool, authoritative, and friendly face. In order to make sure that you are comfortable and well-informed, I would want to go over some essential information before we go on. In BDSM, trust and talking to each other are very important, and I want to make sure we agree.

Elena nods, and her heart is beating fast with joy and worry. She pays close attention as Sophia talks.

As Sophia speaks, her voice is calm and comforting. "Initially and foremost, we will never disrespect each other's boundaries." This room is meant to be fun and open to discovery, but your comfort and safety are the most important things to me.

Sophia picks up a pad bound in leather from a small table next to the bed. She opens it and sees a list of safe words and phrases that everyone agrees on. Each one is carefully chosen to show a different level of comfort and energy. "We'll use safe words to make sure we both feel good and know what the other person needs." They wandered and agreed that the safe word "Scarlet" would be our main safe word. Say "Scarlet" at any time if you feel like you can't handle it anymore or need to stop. Everything will stop right away.

No questions will be asked; your safety and comfort are the most important things.

Elena lets out a big breath and feels calm come over her. "I get it, Sophia." I really like the thoroughness you are.

Sophia smiles and looks like she agrees. "It's very important that we stay in touch during our time together." Do not hesitate to inform me if you feel the need to make modifications or discontinue. We will check in on you from time to time to make sure you are still happy and comfortable.

Sophia points to the different pieces of tools in the room. "This room has everything we might need to learn more about BDSM in different ways." From the bed's shackles to the bondage frame, every part was picked because it works well and is of good quality. I'll show you how to use each piece and answer any questions you have. The goal is to make a place where we can both feel strong and united.

Elena is amazed and excited as she looks around the room. "It's amazing how carefully you set everything up."

Sophia nods, and her face softens. "I think a well-prepared space makes the experience better and lets us focus on connecting and exploring." All of this gear is here to make your journey easier, not to make you feel bad.

Just let me know if you ever need a break or aren't sure what to do.

Chapter 2 BDSM Exploration

Sophia tells Elena about the different parts of BDSM that they will look into. She starts by talking about the bed locks and how they can be changed to make the person more comfortable and in charge. "There are different ways to use the bed's restraints." You can be held in different positions with them, which lets you feel and experience different things. They're padded to keep you comfortable, and you can make changes as needed.

Then she moves on to the bondage frame and shows what it can do. "This frame lets you set up more complex restraints." Remember that we will use it in a way that brings us the most comfort and pleasure. I will always check in with you to make sure everything is okay and to your liking.

Sophia shows the group of whips, paddles, and floggers. "These are tools that can make our sessions better. Each one makes me feel a different way." I'll tell you how each one feels, and then you can choose which ones you want to try. We're going to start out slowly, and you can change things or stop at any time.

She moves to the big mirror and changes how bright it is. It looks nice and is useful that the mirror is here. It lets us see what's going on and improves the viewing experience. We can see each other's responses and faces, which adds another level of closeness.

Sophia looks back at Elena with a serious but sympathetic look on her face. "Trust is the key to a good experience." Have faith in yourself, me, and the way we talk to each other. You should treat this place with respect and care while you enjoy yourself and look around.

Elena takes it all in, feeling both excited and calm at the same time. Sophia's care and dedication to making sure everyone has a safe and enjoyable time are things she values.

Sophia reaches out and lightly touches Elena on the shoulder, which makes her face soften. "I want you to know that this is your experience and not mine." You can always tell me if you need anything or if you feel bad. The most important things are your health and happiness.

Elena smiles and nods, feeling very thankful. "Thank you, Sophia." It makes me feel really at ease and excited to talk about this with you.

Sophia smiles warmly, and the look in her eyes shows that she is both sure of herself and kind. "That makes me happy." Let's take our time, enjoy the process, and make this something we will both never forget.

Since the rules have been made clear and the planning has been done, Elena is excited and ready. Sophia worked hard to make the apartment a place where people could explore and bond. It shows in the carefully chosen features and careful planning that went into it.

Elena feels better because she knows Sophia's knowledge and promise to trust will help her and her friend all the way through their journey to a relationship that will end till death. Elena is ready to fully enjoy the evening, which she thinks will be full of new experiences, closeness, and deep connection. She was ready to explore the thing she wanted for years. She knows that it was not too easy but she was willing to do it. That's why she looked for a dominant that would make her an expert in BDSM.

She walked up to Elena with a soft smile on her face, and her sharp eyes were filled with comfort and love. The woman asked Elena, "Are you ready to start?" in a calm voice.

Elena agreed, but her throat hurt from holding her breath. "Yes, I am," she said, barely raising her voice.

Sophia took Elena by the hand and led her to the middle of the room, where they could play on a soft cushion. Sophia took out some silk rope and said, "Let's start with something easy and gentle." "I desire you to feel protected and at ease each phase of the way."

Sophia skillfully uncoiled the rope, and Elena watched as the material slid easily through her fingers. Elena got a chill up her spine when she saw the rope and thought about what was going to happen.

"Hold out your hands for me," Sophia told them in a tone that was both firm and friendly.

Elena put her hands out in front of her, palms up, and her fingers were slightly shaking. Sophia took her time as she wrapped Elena's arms in the silk rope. Slowly, each knot was put in place, and the silk felt cool and soft against Elena's skin. Sophia's touch was strong but gentle, just the right amount of control and care.

"How does that feel?" Sophia asked with her eyes fixed on Elena's, hoping to see any signs of pain.

She responded, "It feels... wonderful," her voice shaky with excitement. The hard but gentle pressure of the knots and the feeling of the silk against her skin made her more sensual and aroused.

Sophia smiled because she liked Elena's answer. "All right. Remember that you can say our "safe word" whenever you feel uncomfortable or want to stop.

Elena said, "Scarlet," and that was their second choice for a safe word.

"Exactly," Sophia said, and her voice was calm. "You're doing wonderfully, Elena."

Sophia took a step back to admire her job after the wrists of Elena were safely tied. When Sophia saw Elena standing there with the soft, pretty ropes around her wrists, Shez felt both beautiful and vulnerable. Sophia was proud of and loved her new servant, and her heart grew big.

Sophia moved behind Elena and said, "Let's take this one step further." She slowly raised Elena's bound hands above her head and tied the ends of the ropes to a hook in the ceiling.

Elena had to stand with her arms stretched out above her head. Her body was open, and Sophia could hurt her.

"How does this feel?" Sophia asked as she lightly put her hands on Elena's shoulders.

Elena took a big breath and felt how her arms were stretched out and how vulnerable she was. She said, "It feels... intense," and her voice shook with fear and joy.

Sophia whispered, "Good," and her lips touched Elena's ear. "I want you to trust me, let go, and enjoy the feelings." "You're safe with me."

Sophia's hands moved over Elena's body and touched her in a hard, measured way. She lightly ran her fingers over Elena's arms, down her sides, and across her back, making her feel good all over. Elena shivered, and her body was eager to feel Sophia's touch.

When Sophia whispered to Elena, "Your skin is so sensitive," her breath felt warm against her neck. "Every touch, every caress, is magnified when you're bound like this."

Elena let out a soft moan. Being bound made her senses stronger. Every time Sophia touched her or breathed, she could feel it. She found herself getting more and more into the experience as it made her feel vulnerable and aroused at the same time.

Sophia lowered her hands and ran them over Elena's hips and legs. "You have such a beautiful body," Sophia said in a low voice. "I'd like to feel every part of you and find all the ways I can make you happy. There are many things from your head to toe. Your hips are round and soft. That could make anyone fall for you, man or woman."

Sophia's hands touched the bottom of Elena's dress, and Elena's breath caught. Sophia began to remove the fabric slowly and carefully, leaving a little more Elena's skin breath in the cool air. It was exciting and fearful at the same time, and Elena's heart was racing with excitement.

"Elena, do you believe in me?" Sophia asked in a strong but soft voice.

"Yes," Elena said, and her voice was full of determination. "I trust you completely."

Sophia kept lifting Elena's dress with a smile on her face. She did it slowly, and the dress touched Elena's whole body. Sophia finally got it over her head and let it fall to the ground. Elena stood in front of her in nothing but her pants. Her body was shaking with fear and excitement.

Sophia took a step back to take in the view. "You're beautiful! Look at your curves! Oh my God, your soft and round hips, your breasts, your vagina—everything shines," she said with real awe in her voice. "Thank you for trusting me with your body, Elena."

Elena blushed when she was complimented. Her cheeks turned red with both shame and happiness. "Thank you for showing me the way," she said in a voice that was almost whisper.

Sophia moved closer to Elena and ran her hands over her body again. This time, she touched Elena more carefully, running her fingers along the lines of her pants to tease the pussy underneath. Elena gasped at the feeling, and her body naturally arched towards Sophia's touch.

Sophia whispered, "You're so responsive," and her lips touched Elena's neck. "It's beautiful to see."

When Sophia put her hands on Elena's breasts, she skillfully unhooked her bra and let it fall off. She looked at Elena's skin slowly, her touch being both hard and soft. Elena let out a soft moan, and her body shook with pleasure. The moment made her happy and scared at the same time.

"Does this feel good?" Sophia asked, her voice was low and sultry.

"Yes, That's excellent, Sophia." Elena took deep breaths and closed her eyes as she let herself feel what was going on. "It feels incredible."

Sophia smiled because she liked Elena's answer. "All right. I want you to feel everything, let go, and enjoy the thrill.

Sophia's hands kept looking around and moved down to Elena's pants. She slid them down Elena's legs slowly and carefully, leaving her completely naked. With Sophia now in charge of her whole body, Elena shivered as the cool air hit her.

"You're beautiful," Sophia told her with a voice full of adoration. "I want you to feel unique emotions." We'll look into things you didn't even think of.

Sophia's words made Elena's heart race, and her body hurt with excitement. Sophia had her full trust, and Elena knew she was safe with her. She found herself getting more and more into the experience as the mix of weakness and desire got stronger.

Sophia put her hands on Elena's hips and touched her without being too soft. She was slowly feeling her way over Elena's whole body. Sophia fell in love with Elena because of her soft, smooth body. "I'm going to tie your legs now," she said in a calm voice. "I want you to feel secure and grounded."

Elena gave a short, sharp nod as she waited for Sophia to do something next. Sophia took out another piece of silk rope and started to wrap it around Elena's legs. The soft stuff looked very different from the tight knots. She took her time and made sure that each knot was strong but not too tight. Elena felt both bound and at ease afterward.

"How does that feel?" Sophia asked, looking at Elena's face to see if she looked like she was in pain. "Just say our safe word if you feel scared or uncomfortable." "Remember what our safe word was?" She also said.

"Of course, Scarlet, I remember that," Elena replied.

Along with "It feels... good," Elena said, her voice shaking from fear and joy. When the soft pressure of the ropes against her skin made her feel bound, it was both scary and soothing.

Sophia smiled because she liked Elena's answer. "Elena, you're doing great. Trust me and let go."

Being sure that Elena's legs were tied down, Sophia took a step back to admire her job. When she saw Elena standing there with soft, pretty ropes around her body, she felt both beautiful and vulnerable. Sophia was proud of and loved her new servant, and her heart grew enormous.

Sophia moved to a nearby table and picked up a small, fancy candle. "Now let's take this a step further," she said. The soft light from the lit wick gave the room a warm glow.

Elena looked with wide eyes and a lot of excitement in her heart. She had never done wax play before, and the thought of it scared and excited her at the same time.

"Have you ever tried wax play before?" Sophia asked with a tone that was both soft and firm.

Elena shook her head and took short, sharp breaths. "No, I've never tried it."

Sophia gave an encouraging smile. "It's a great way to learn about feeling and being in charge." It can be very exciting to feel the heat and how it cools off your skin.

Elena said yes, and her heart was racing with fear and joy. "I'm ready to try."

Sophia moved closer with a strong grip on the candle. "Remember, if at any point you feel uncomfortable or want to stop, just say our safe word."

"Scarlet," Elena said again, confirming that they had picked the right word.

Sophia smiled and nodded, and her eyes were filled with love and comfort. "Elena, you're in good hands. Believe me.

Sophia tilted the candle with a steady hand, letting a small drop of wax land on Elena's shoulder. The heat of the wax gave Elena a rush of pleasure that happened right away and was very strong.

Elena let out a gasp, and her body arched naturally towards the feeling. The heat was both frightening and thrilling, very different from the room's cool air.

"How does that feel?" Sophia asked with her eyes fixed on Elena's, hoping to see any signs of pain.

"It's amazing," Elena said, but her voice was short with happiness and shock. The hot wax cooling on her skin made her feel a wonderful mix of pain and joy. It was a new feeling she was excited to learn more about.

Sophia smiled because she liked how Elena responded. She said, "Good," in a low, seductive whisper. "Let's explore this sensation together."

Sophia carefully turned the candle over again, letting another drop of wax land on Elena's other shoulder. Elena's first response was a sharp intake of breath, followed by a low moan from her neck. The electric shock of the hot wax mixed with the cool wax sent chills down her spine.

Sophia kept letting the wax drip onto Elena's body. Each drop was a planned act of both joy and pain. From Elena's shoulders to her chest and then to her stomach, each spot made her feel something different. Every time a drop fell, Elena's body writhed, and her mind got lost in the flood of feelings.

Sophia said in a soft voice, "You're doing so well, Elena." Her breath felt good against Elena's ear. "Just let go and feel."

Elena's mind was full of different feelings and sensations. She had never felt so open and fragile, but also so very alive. Every drop of wax and touch from Sophia seemed to make her feel even better. Every touch and whisper of breath felt like they were a hundred times stronger against her skin.

Sophia put the candle down and picked up a feather. The feather's soft, delicate touch was very different from the wax's rough feel. Starting at Elena's neck and slowly moving down her body, she lightly traced the feather over her. The feather's touch was so light that it was almost annoying. It hurt so much that Elena could barely breathe.

Feather was drawing her body from the neck to the breasts, the stomach, and the pussy. Going through the pussy made Elena's body feel very excited. Because the feather felt good on her body, she was thrilled and her body was shaking. Sophia used that feather to find out every part of Elena.

"Do you like this?" Sophia asked with a voice that was both interesting and serious.

"Yes," Elena gasped, and her whole body shook with excitement. "It feels incredible, more intensive."

Sophia smiled because she liked Elena's answer. Her touch was light and sexy, going from Elena's neck to her breasts and then down to her stomach and legs as she teased her with the feather. Elena's body quickly reacted, and her skin pricked up with pain.

"Such a responsive little submissive," Sophia said in a voice filled with praise. "You're perfect, Elena."

Sophia put the feather down and picked up a flogger. The blade's many tails made her think of a different kind of pain. Before giving Elena a light swat on the thigh to tease her, she ran the flogger lightly over her skin so she could feel its weight and feel how it felt.

Elena let out a gasp and arched her back toward the flogger. It stung hard for a short time, giving you a taste of what was to come. Sophia kept giving Elena slight, playful swats on the body, each one a carefully balanced mix of pain and joy.

"How does that feel?" Sophia asked in a strong but soft voice.

She said, "It feels... intense," and her voice shook with fear and joy. "But good. Wonderful."

Sophia responded, "That's what I like to hear," she was happy to hear it. It got harder for her to hit Elena with the flogger's tails, which left tiny red marks on her skin. Every hit makes her legs shake. The swats turned her soft, pretty legs red. Elena's moans got louder, and her body started to shake from pain and joy.

"Such a good girl," Sophia said in a soft, comforting voice. "Eleanor, you're doing great. Feel and let go."

As Sophia kept using the flogger, Elena's mind slipped even more into a state of happy surrender. She felt every hit and touch so strongly that it made her gasp for air. The pleasure and pain mixed together so well that she got lost in a storm of emotions.

Sophia put down the flogger and grabbed a blindfold. She gently put it over Elena's eyes. "I'm going to blindfold you now," she said, and the sound of her voice was calming. "This will make your other abilities stronger. Believe me.

Sophia put the blindfold over Elena's eyes with soft but strong hands. The soft cloth fell over her eyes and made her feel very dark.

Elena took a short breath, and her thoughts turned to the sounds and feelings that were about to happen. When she lost her sight, her other abilities got stronger. Every touch and word became more noticeable.

"Can you see anything?" Elena got chills when she heard Sophia's low, seductive purr.

"No," Elena said in a voice that was almost a whisper.

"Good," Sophia said, and her voice was a mix of confidence and direction. "Listen to my voice. Believe me.

Elena nodded, and her heart started beating faster in excitement. Sophia's hands felt so light that they made her skin tingle as they moved over her arms. Sophia spoke, and her breath felt warm against her ear. Each word was a promise that made her mouth water.

"I will keep you safe. "Just let go."

Sophia's fingers moved back and forth over Elena's shoulders, making tiny patterns on her back. She felt lightning shocks of pleasure all over her body when he touched her. Elena's feelings were sharpened, and each touch felt deeper and more powerful. Sophia's heat, the faint smell of her perfume, and the sound of her breath were all things she could feel.

Sophia moved her hands down and lightly touched Elena's vagina. She let out a soft moan and arched her back to be touched.

Sophia's lips touched her neck and kissed her softly, making her shiver. It was almost too much to handle to guess where Sophia would touch next and how she would tease and bother her.

"You like that, don't you?" Sophia whispered, and her lips touched Elena's ear.

Elena breathed out "Yes," her voice shaking with desire.

Sophia's hands kept exploring, and her touch was both soft and firm. It made Elena gasp when she teased the curves of her breasts and ran her fingers along the sensitive peaks. All of a sudden, Elena's world was filled with sounds and feelings, and every touch and whisper was a note in the tune of joy.

Sophia said, "You're really doing wonderfully," and her voice was like a sense of relief. "I'll take care of you, you just have to relax."

Because of Sophia's touch, Elena's body reacted, and her skin began to burn with need. The blindfold made her feel more aroused and vulnerable at the same time. Sophia moved her hands lower, feeling her hips and legs to see how they bend and how soft they are. It was clear that every touch was meant to bring Elena closer to the edge.

That word, "Please," was Elena's plea for more.

"Patience, my love," Sophia answered, her voice full of joy. "I'm going to give you everything you need, but on my behalf."

Sophia spoke in a low and deep voice, "I'll make you feel things you've never felt before."

Sophia kissed Elena on the lips, it was gentle, soft, and long, and it made her feel better, her heart raced. There was no end to the ways Sophia touched and felt her body. She let out a gasp when she felt a sharp sting on her breast, followed by a gentle touch.

Elena moaned, "Sophia," and leaned forward to touch Sophia.

Sophia laughed once more, and her fingers kept exploring. Elena could feel a flogger's cool metal against her skin. The soft leather tails touched her breasts, stomach, and legs. She could feel her body shaking with need as the heat built up inside her.

She begged Sophia, "Please," and her voice was barely above a whisper.

Sophia's only reaction was a soft laugh, and her fingers kept hurting her. Elena could feel the stress rising up inside her; her body begged to be freed. Sophia's soft, seductive voice was against her ear, and she could feel her breath.

Sophia said in a whisper, "Not yet, my love." "Not yet."

Elena moaned, and her body shook with need. Sophia's fingers were pulling at her and teasing her inside her vagina. The release was building up inside her, and she could feel her body tensing up.

She begged Sophia, "Please," Elena said in a frantic voice.

Sophia wouldn't say anything but a soft laugh, and her fingers kept attacking. Elena could feel herself getting ready for an orgasm; her body was shaking with desire. Sophia's lips were on hers, and the soft, long kiss made her

heart race.

Chapter 3 The Pleasure

Elena's senses were sharpened by the blindfold, and Sophia's touch became the most important thing in her world. Another length of silk rope was tied around her feet and to the ground, squeezing her legs together. The soft bands around her hands held them above her head, leaving her body exposed and defenseless. Every time Sophia touched or spoke, Elena felt lightning sparks go through her body.

Sophia lightly and lightly ran her fingers down Elena's vagina. Elena was so scared that her body was shaking, and she took short, weak breaths. The soft noise of the city outside and her fast breathing filled the room, making it feel close and romantic. She felt pleasure everywhere in the room.

Sophia put a warm breath in Elena's ear and said, "I want you to focus on my touch." "Let go of everything else and just feel."

Elena answered with a quiet whisper. Being blind made her senses sharper. She could feel Sophia's fingers moving and her breath making a faint sound against her skin. Being in that feeling, which was a tempting mix of desire and weakness, made her lose herself.

Sophia picked up a very small and thin vibrator from a table next to hers. As she put it on Elena's skin and turned it on, a soft hum filled the room. As she slowly stroked Elena's breasts, she felt shivers of pleasure run down her spine. Her body was trembling and vibrating due to the pleasure made by the vibrator on her body.

"How does that feel?" Sophia asked in an enticing, whispery voice.

With a breath, Elena curved her body towards the feeling and said, "Incredible." She wanted more because the movements were both soft and strong in a way that looked appealing.

Sophia smiled because she liked Elena's answer. "Okay. "I want you to feel everything, let go, and enjoy every moment."

Elena's nipples were teased as she ran the vibrator over her body and slid it down her stomach. Every touch was meant to make Elena feel very horny. The soft hum of the vibrator, the smooth silk ropes, and Sophia's skillful fingers were all too much. She made her horny with each and every touch.

Sophia bent down and used the vibrator to touch Elena's inner legs, being careful not to touch her most sensitive areas. Elena's heart raced with desire, and she gasped for air. She let out a quiet whimper and thrust her hips towards the feeling. The excitement was almost too much for her to handle. She felt as if she was going to cum and pee all over. But it was the feeling of pleasure.

A strong but kind voice said, "Patience," from Sophia. "I want to take my time with you."

Elena moaned again, her body aching with a need. The steady, intentional teasing was getting stronger and stronger until it overwhelmed her. Sophia was taking care of her, and she had full faith in her, but the tension was almost too much for her to handle.

Sophia kept making fun of and teasing Elena with the vibrator, getting it to her weakest spots but never giving her the comfort she needed so badly. As she was being tortured, her mouth watered, and she shook and gasped in both pleasure and pain.

Sophia finally put the vibrator on Elena's clitoris, and she let out a sharp gasp at how strong it felt. Both the soft and strong feelings made her feel waves of pleasure all over her body.

Sophia said with a tone of thanks, "You're really responding." "It's beautiful to see."

She let out a deep sigh and curved her body towards the feeling. As Sophia's skilled hands mixed with the waves, she was swept away by the feelings. All of her senses were filled with bliss.

Sophia kept using the vibrator and she moved slowly and carefully. It got tense with each touch as she took her time to make Elena feel close to happiness and keep her there.

Elena let out short breaths as her body shook with fear. The strong feeling was almost too much for her to handle; it flooded her senses. With the mask and ropes on, every touch and caress felt stronger to her.

"Do you trust me, Elena?" Sophia asked in a firm but friendly way.

Elena said, "Yes," and her voice was sure. "I trust you completely."

Sophia's smile was naughty as she kept making fun of and bothering Elena, using the vibrator over and over to bring her close to happiness. She felt such a strong mix of happiness and pain that she could not breathe or stand still.

Sophia was very skilled as her fingers could spot the right place to be seduced and pressed to take her submissive at the edge of pleasure, which made Elena get mad for the desire and the pleasure. The strong feeling, which was a mix of happiness and irritation, made her gasp for air and fall to the ground shaking. Her body was under so much stress that she almost couldn't handle it.

Sophia kept moving her fingers around with fine dexterity. Her touches were firm and purposeful. Elena was breathless and was moaning continuously, she had never experienced this type of pleasure in her whole life. Sophia made it come true in her presence.

"You're so close," Sophia said softly. "I feel it. Take a deep breath and enjoy the present moment.

Elena let out a loud moan, and her body shook with need.

For some reason, she was so happy that it affected every part of her body. With the mask and ropes on, every touch and caress felt stronger to her.

Sophia kept moving her fingers. She was rubbing her pussy while the vibrator was on her clitoris. Her touches were firm and purposeful. Elena was full of feeling, joy, pleasure, and desire at the same time. She proceeded to torment Elena by switching between the vibrator and her expert hands in order to do so. Elena gasped and moaned with pleasure as she touched her breasts and pinched and rolled her nipples between her fingers. Elena was going crazy from all the different feelings. Her body was shaking with need.

Sophia then grabbed for a glass dildo. The cool surface of the dildo was very different from Elena's hot skin. She put it up against Elena's vagina and teased her with the tip before slowly pushing it in. Elena's back rose, and she let out a happy cry.

"That's it, my pet," Sophia said in a low voice. "Take it all."

She moved slowly and carefully as she put and took out the dildo. Elena's cries got louder, and her body writhed against the chains. Sophia added the vibrator back into the mix and pressed it against Elena's clit while she kept her dildo pushed inside her.

It was almost too much for Elena to handle all of these feelings at once. She was on the edge, just on the edge of having an orgasm. Every nerve ending was on fire with pleasure. Sophia's speech, touch, and the way the toys inside her felt were all too much and not enough at the same time.

Sophia knew Elena was close by. She leaned

in close to Elena and blew hot air into her ear. "Are you ready to come for me, my pet?" She spoke softly.

Elena needed to orgasm badly. But Sophia still wants to tease her. She set aside the vibrator and a glass dildo. And picked up another dildo from the bag full of various sex toys and she put it into Elena's mouth. Elena was shocked at first but then she realized that this was something made of plastic.

"You scared?" Sophia asked.

"A little bit," Elena chuckled.

Sophia asked her to suck the dildo first. As Elena started sucking the dildo, Sophia picked another toy from her toy's bag. It was a small anal bead for the extension of the pleasure.

"Do you still believe in me, Elena?" Sophia asked Elena.

Elena replied, "Of course, Sophia."

"Are you ready for something extra to extend your pleasure?" Sophia questioned.

"I'm always ready, Sophia" she replied.

Sophia gently slides the anal bead into Elena's vagina. Elena let out a moan. The pain and the pleasure both made her moan while sucking the dildo. Sophia takes the dildo from Elena's mouth. She spread her legs to give her a good view and slowly started rubbing the head of the dildo against her wet hole. Gently sliding into her pussy, she let out a moan as this new toy filled her up.

Sophia's firm but gentle touch finally brought Elena to the edge of happiness again. Elena was feeling so many strong emotions at once that she could not breathe or stand still. With the mask and ropes on, every touch and caress felt stronger to her. Sophia had to put her leg over her shoulder to prevent Elena from kicking her as she continued to pound her pussy. But suddenly Sophia stopped and left Elina trembling with desire. Sophia finally sped up things and sent Elena into a shattered orgasm, which released all the stress that had been building up. Elena was silent and ecstatic. She was shaking from how intense the meeting was; the pleasure was a mix of all her senses. Sophia's gentle and firm touches and her grip on the BDSM made it easy to know it, for Elena.

Sophia held Elena close and soothed and praised her. "You did so well," she told Elena, her breath warm on her ear. "I'm so proud of you."

Sophia carefully took Elena's legs and wrists off and took the ropes off. She took Elena in her arms and took off the blindfold, letting it fall to the ground. The two women lay down together on the plush rug, their bodies tangled in a web of love and desire.

Elena said, "Thank you," and her voice was full of thanks. "That was incredible."

Sophia smiled, and her eyes were filled with love and warmth. She said in a soft voice, "I appreciate your trust in me." "It was my pleasure."

Sophia smiled, and her eyes were filled with love and warmth. In a cool and kind voice, she told him, "You did great." "I'm so proud of you."

As the last sounds of their shared pleasure faded into the night, the room went from being filled with the intense fire of desire to being filled with peace and quiet. Sophia and Elena's soft, forced breaths mixed with the silence. Their bodies shone with the glow of their passionate exploration.

Elena broke into a smile, and her earlier worries seemed like a long time ago. "Thank you for showing me the way," she said in a soft voice. "I've never felt anything like this before."

Elena felt safe and comforted as Sophia wrapped her arms around her. They were lying on the bed together, their bodies touching. The heat of their desire was still strong between them. Sophia touched Elena on the back in relaxing patterns. Her touch was a quiet promise of safety and care.

In the quiet that followed, their breaths slowly started to match, a small sign of how well they were getting along. Sophia spoke kind words and support into Elena's ear. Her voice was soothing and took away any worries or questions that were still there.

When Elena closed her eyes, her body relaxed even more in Sophia's arms. She told her, "I felt safe with you," and her voice was barely above a whisper. "I've never felt so free to explore my desires."

Elena smiled and pressed her face against Sophia's neck "I want more of this," she said. "I want to keep exploring with you."

Sophia's smile got bigger, and she wanted the same thing Elena did. "We'll have plenty of time for that," she told her. "This is just the beginning."

As the night turned into early morning, neither of them felt the need to sleep. Instead, they enjoyed the warmth of their closeness, with their bodies and minds moving together in a chorus of happiness and satisfaction.

Elena broke the calm silence with a thoughtful voice. "I've always been curious about this world, but I never knew how to start."

Sophia's fingers kept moving along Elena's back, making her feel better. "Being interested is the first step," she said softly. "It's important to find someone you trust, someone who understands your boundaries and desires."

Elena looked up at her with a bold look in her eyes. "I need to find out more." I'd like to know what makes this so strong.

Their night together was a discovery that showed how strong their wants were. As they lay in each other's arms with the sun rising outside, they knew this was just the start of their journey together.

Over the next few days and weeks, Sophia and Elena kept exploring the depths of their desires. They tried out different parts of

BDSM, always putting communication and trust first. Every new thing they did brought them closer together, making the bond they made stronger.

They learned about the beauty of both control and surrender as they worked through the complicated relationships of power. They loved the feelings and sensations that their meetings made them feel. They liked the balance between being in charge and letting go.

Elena's confidence grew as she tried new things and learned more about what she wanted. She discovered a strength she had never known before when she gave up herself. Sophia also felt good about herself when she was in charge of Elena. Her dominant side was tamed by a strong sense of care and duty.

THE END

Dear reader,

Thank you for reading to the end!

If you want more short stories, check out my popular series *Hooked by the BBC*.

Amber

www.ingramcontent.com/pod-product-compliance
Lightning Source LLC
LaVergne TN
LVHW041631070526
838199LV00052B/3314